Lemonade Raid

"I don't know who took your lemons," Ned told Nancy. "And stop bothering me!"

"We didn't do anything to you!" Nancy shouted.

Ned spun around. "Remember the dogs I was walking this morning?" he asked. "They were so wet and muddy from jumping in the lake after your puppy that the owner fired me. Now I'm losing a dollar a day because of you!"

"That's terrible," Bess said. "But it wasn't our fault."

Ned quickly walked along the street with the four little poodles. Halfway down the block, he bent down to untangle the dogs' leashes. When he straightened up, Nancy gasped. A bunch of lemon slices had fallen right out of his shirt pocket.

"He's got our lemons!" George cried. "Let's get him!"

The Nancy Drew Notebooks

Available from MINSTREL Books

#19

THE NANCY DREW NOTEBOOKS®

THE LEMONADE RAID

CAROLYN KEENE

Illustrated by Anthony Accardo

A MINSTREL® BOOK

PUBLISHED BY POCKET BOOKS

New York   London   Toronto   Sydney   Tokyo   Singapore

A MINSTREL PAPERBACK *Original*

 A Minstrel Book published by
POCKET BOOKS, a division of Simon & Schuster Inc.
1230 Avenue of the Americas, New York, NY 10020

Copyright © 1997 by Simon & Schuster Inc.
Produced by Mega-Books, Inc.

ISBN: 0-671-56863-9

First Minstrel Books printing July 1997

10 9 8 7 6 5 4 3 2 1

NANCY DREW, THE NANCY DREW NOTEBOOKS, A MINSTREL BOOK and colophon are registered trademarks of Simon & Schuster Inc.

Cover art by Aleta Jenks

Printed in the U.S.A.

THE LEMONADE RAID

1

Lemonade and Bugs

Let's open it!" eight-year-old Nancy Drew said as the deliveryman plunked a big brown box on the porch.

Hannah Gruen, the Drews' housekeeper, signed for the mysterious package. It was addressed to "The Drew Family."

"Hurry up," George Fayne said, helping Nancy remove the tape.

Bess Marvin knelt beside her cousin George. She watched as Nancy pulled off the lid of the box.

The three best friends looked inside and frowned. "Lemons?" they all said at once.

1

George sat back on her heels. "I thought it was going to be something good."

"Why would someone send us all these lemons?" Nancy asked Hannah.

"Well, my little sourpuss," Hannah teased, "they're from your father's friend Frank Wilson, who lives in California. Here's a note saying they come from the lemon trees in his backyard. I guess he didn't know what to do with all of them." Hannah looked down at the lemons. "I can make a few pies, but I don't know what to do with the rest, either."

"We could make lemonade," Nancy said.

Bess licked her lips. "That sounds yummy."

"Yeah," George agreed. "It's really hot today. Hey, I know," she said after a moment. "We can set up a lemonade stand in the park. It'll be fun!"

That night Nancy's father gave Nancy permission to use the lemons Hannah didn't need. The next morning

Bess and George came over to Nancy's house early to make the lemonade and a small sign for their stand.

"Phew." Bess brushed her blond bangs away from her face after they'd been working for a while. "I didn't think making lemonade would be such hard work."

"We must have squeezed a zillion lemons," George said, "and we only have a little bit of juice." She looked at the pitcher. "I wonder what it tastes like."

"I'll bet it's really sour," Nancy said, puckering her lips. "We haven't added the water or sugar yet."

"I want to try it anyway." George poured herself a small cup. She drank some of the juice and grinned at Bess. "I kind of like it."

Bess grabbed another lemon and cut it in half to squeeze. "That figures."

After the girls had finished making the lemonade, they piled everything they needed for the stand into Nancy's old red wagon—a small card table and a pink tablecloth, the juicer and extra sugar, paper cups and a big green pitcher.

"Don't forget the lemons," George said, carefully putting the box on top of everything else.

Then Nancy's puppy, Chocolate Chip, raced out of the garage. She was holding her leash in her mouth and wagging her shiny brown tail.

"Come on, Chip." Nancy snapped on her dog's leash. "You can help us sell lemonade."

The girls and Chip walked along, pulling the wagon behind them. It was a hot summer morning, perfect for selling lemonade. But when they reached the park, they got a horrible surprise.

Brenda Carlton and Alison Wegman were headed their way. And it looked as if they were going to set up a lemonade stand, too. Even worse, Alison was carrying a much bigger sign than theirs. It said Fresh Squeezed Lemonade and had bright yellow lemons and butterfly stickers all around the edges.

4

"This stinks," Bess grumbled as Nancy and George picked a spot near the water fountain and opened up the folding table.

Then Brenda and Alison marched over.

"Copycats!" Brenda said in a loud, nasty voice.

"We are not!" Bess shouted.

"Are, too!" Alison shouted back. "We were here first!"

"Were not," George said.

Brenda gave Nancy a long, hard look. "Why don't you go somewhere else?" she said.

"We can sell lemonade here, too, if we want." Nancy turned away from her and put the final touches on the stand.

"Who cares about them anyway?" Brenda said to Alison. "We have a much better stand, and better lemonade, too."

"That's what *you* think," George said.

Nancy turned around. "I bet we'll sell tons more than you do."

"No way," Alison huffed.

"*Yes* way," Bess said back.

"Oh, yeah? Let's have a contest," Brenda said. "We'll sell each cup for twenty-five cents. Whoever sells the most lemonade by tomorrow at five o'clock wins."

"And the loser has to do anything the winner says," Nancy added.

"Good idea." Brenda laughed. "We'll probably make you all eat bugs when *we* win!"

"Or maybe something even *worse*," Alison said.

"Why don't you both make like a tree and leave!" George yelled.

With that, Alison and Brenda went back to their stand, and Nancy, Bess, and George sat down on the ground to wait for their first customer.

"Hey, girls." Bobby Alden came over to their stand with a big smile. "I have to buy some lemonade from my favorite ice-cream nuts." Bobby was fourteen and worked part-time with his grandfather, Sid Alden, at the Double Dip. It was Nancy's favorite ice-cream shop.

Soon Nancy, Bess, and George were

pouring lemonade for a long line of people.

Rebecca Ramirez stopped by and bought some. She said it tasted great.

Mike Minelli, David Berger, and Jason Hutchings each bought a glass after their baseball game. Then the rest of their team came over. When things slowed down, George started to call people over to their table.

"Want to buy some more lemonade, Bobby?" George asked when Bobby Alden passed their stand again. This time his hair was wet from swimming in the lake.

"Gotta get to work," he said, rushing away.

Then Nancy saw Ned Nickerson. He was walking three big dogs that were barking and pulling him in all different directions.

"Want a cup of our lemonade?" George called out.

"Sure," Ned said, dragging the dogs over to the stand.

Nancy carefully poured a cup. Bess

giggled as Ned's dogs stuck their noses in the box and began pulling lemons out with their teeth.

"Look! Your dogs think our lemons are toys," Bess said, trying to take the lemons away. But the harder she tried, the harder the dogs tugged. One dog chomped on a lemon and squirted juice all over Bess's T-shirt.

"Yechh!" Bess shouted.

"Hey, we need those," George scolded the dogs, pulling the box away from them. But the dogs followed the box and stuck their faces into it again. George sighed and looked at Ned. "Why do you have so many dogs, anyway?"

Ned tried to wrestle a lemon away from a golden retriever. "I'm walking dogs for the summer. People pay me to do it," he said, finally getting the lemon out of the dog's mouth. He tossed it on the ground.

The golden retriever grabbed another lemon and put his front paws on the table.

"Down," Ned said. But the dog didn't budge.

Nancy giggled. "It looks like the dogs are walking *you.*"

"They know who's boss," Ned insisted, pulling the retriever down from the table. Then the three dogs bolted toward the lake, dragging Ned with them.

"Sure they do," George called after him.

The three girls couldn't stop laughing.

But then Chip broke loose from the table and ran after Ned and his dogs.

"Come back!" Nancy shouted. She tried to catch up, but her puppy was too fast. Then Ned's dogs got away from him and started running after Chip.

"Help!" Bess screamed as the big dogs raced toward Nancy's puppy.

Then the three dogs' leashes got snarled around a big oak tree.

"Quick! Get them!" Ned yelled, but he was too late.

The dogs got loose again and chased Chip over to the lake. Nancy almost caught Chip just as her puppy jumped into the water. The three other dogs followed.

Ned waded in and grabbed his dogs' leashes. His pants were sopping wet.

"Your pooch is a real pest!" Ned yelled. He pulled his dogs out of the lake and stomped off with them.

"Boy, Ned's pretty mad," George said when she and Bess caught up with Nancy and Chip. The chocolate Labrador retriever had wandered out of the lake and stopped to drink water from a puddle.

"I know." Nancy scooped up her panting puppy. "You are a very naughty doggy!" she scolded Chocolate Chip.

Nancy carried Chip back to the lemonade stand and tied her leash to the table leg. She watched Chip sniff the squished lemon Ned had thrown on the ground earlier.

That was when Nancy noticed something.

"Oh, no!" she cried. "We're going to have to eat bugs!"

2

Looking for Lemons

What are you talking about, Nancy?"
George asked.

"Our box of lemons is gone," Nancy
said, looking at the spot where the box
had been. "We can't make lemonade
without them. And you know what
that means."

"Bugs!" Bess flopped down on the
grass. "Brenda and Alison are going to
win the contest."

"We have to find that box, or else,"
Nancy said.

But the box was nowhere to be
found. They looked everyplace. They

even asked some people in the park, but no one had seen it.

"I didn't even get to drink any of our lemonade," Nancy grumbled. She looked over at Brenda and Alison. Lots of kids were standing around their table, sipping lemonade. Brenda had a jar full of quarters.

Nancy, Bess, and George started taking down their stand.

"I bet *they* took them," Bess said with a nod at Brenda and Alison's table.

"Why are you guys leaving?" Brenda called from her table. "Giving up already?"

"Like you don't know our lemons were stolen," George called back.

"Why would we want *your* lemons?" Alison said. "You touched them. Now they all have cooties."

Brenda and Alison started laughing.

George clenched her fists. "Ooooh, they make me so mad."

"Come on, George," Nancy said sadly. "Let's get out of here."

With Chip trotting beside them, the girls pulled their packed wagon back to Nancy's house and put it in the garage. Then they took the lemonade pitcher into the kitchen and went up to Nancy's room.

Nancy flopped onto her bed and sighed. "I need ice cream," she said to her two best friends.

"Me, too," Bess agreed.

"I guess it couldn't hurt," George added.

A short while later they were standing under the red, white, and green striped awning of the Double Dip. They went inside and sat down at a small wooden table near the window.

"I always think better when I'm at the Double Dip," Nancy said as she pulled out a small notebook and pen from her shorts pocket. Her father had given her the notebook to help her solve mysteries. "We have to find those lemons so we can finish the contest."

"But Brenda's probably sold a million cups by now," Bess said. "And we're going to have to . . ." Bess's voice trailed off.

"But, Bess," George said, smiling. "You might like the taste." She leaned back and pretended to dangle a creepy, crawly bug above her mouth. Then she dropped it in and made fake crunching noises as she slowly chewed.

Nancy laughed.

"Gross!" Bess said. "This is the worst thing that could ever happen!"

"Bess is right." Nancy opened her notebook to a new page. "There's no way I'm going to let Brenda and Alison win the contest. We're going to find those lemons."

First she wrote, "The Missing Lemons Mystery." On the next line she added the word "Suspects."

George sighed. "We already know who stole our lemons—Brenda and Alison."

"You're right, George." Nancy snapped her notebook shut. "They want to win the contest, and Brenda's mean enough to steal our lemons." She looked at the shiny blue cover of her notebook. "But . . ."

"But what?" Bess asked.

"But my father always says to keep a cool head and not to jump to conclusions."

Nancy opened her notebook again and wrote down Brenda's and Alison's names. "There were a lot of people in that park. Anybody could have done it."

"Like who?" George asked.

"Maybe Ned's dogs did it," Bess said after a moment. "They really liked playing with our lemons."

Nancy wrote the word "Dogs" on her list and thought for a minute. "But how could they?" she asked. "Dogs can't pick up a whole box." Nancy scratched the dogs off her list. "I think we're looking for people suspects, not dog suspects."

"What about Ned?" George said.

Nancy put Ned's name on her list. "He *was* really mad at me."

"But Ned's so nice," Bess said. "Um, for a boy, I mean."

"That doesn't mean he didn't do it," Nancy said.

"But even if we figure out who took our lemons, how are we going to get them back?" George asked.

"And in time to win the contest?" Bess added.

Nancy closed her eyes for a minute and thought about the icky bug she was going to have to eat if they didn't win.

"Why so gloomy, ladies?"

Nancy opened her eyes and saw Sid Alden standing by their table. He smiled at them. Nancy thought he looked just like Santa Claus, but without a beard.

"It's such a pretty day," Sid said.

Nancy heaved a big sigh, which was quickly followed by bigger sighs from Bess and George.

"Oh, this sounds pretty bad," Sid said. "Wait, I have a surprise for you girls."

"A surprise!" Nancy said excitedly.

"Yes," Sid said. "But you have to close your eyes and promise not to open them until I tell you to."

"We promise!" Nancy, Bess, and George closed their eyes right away.

"I love surprises!" Bess giggled.

"Shh," George said.

A minute later Nancy heard the *plop, plop, plop* of three cups being set down on the table.

"Okay!" Sid said. "Open!"

The girls opened their eyes to find they each had a scoop of creamy yellow ice cream in front of them.

"On the house," Sid said, beaming. "I thought a free sample of my special flavor of the week would cheer you right up."

Nancy thought Sid was the nicest man on earth—and probably the best ice-cream maker ever.

"Thanks, Sid!" all three girls said together.

As Sid went back to the counter to wait on a customer, Nancy, Bess, and George each took a mouthful.

"You know what?" George said. "This tastes just like . . ."

"I know!" Nancy gasped.

"You don't think . . ." Bess said.

Then Nancy looked over at Sid, who was standing by the cash register. Above him was a sign:

Special Flavor of the Week
Lemonade Supreme

3

Doggy Trouble

"T his is a clue!" George exclaimed.
"I'll bet Sid Alden took our lemons."

"Not Sid Alden," Nancy whispered.

"He must have needed a ton of them
to make lemonade supreme ice cream,"
Bess said.

"But why would he take ours?"
Nancy asked.

"Maybe he was afraid people would
buy our lemonade instead of his ice
cream," Bess said.

Hmm, Nancy thought. Everyone
who had tasted their lemonade had
said it was great. She wrote Sid's

name on her list of suspects. Then she looked up.

"But what if lemonade supreme isn't made with real lemons?" Nancy said hopefully. She didn't want to believe that Sid could be a suspect.

"There's only one way to find out," George whispered. "Ask Sid."

Nancy waited until Sid wasn't busy. Then she walked up to the counter.

"This is one of your best ice-cream flavors," she said cheerfully to Sid. "It almost beats fudge ripple."

"I'm glad you like it," Sid said with a smile. "I've been selling a lot of it. Everyone loves the taste of lemonade in the summer."

"Did you use real lemons to make it?" Nancy asked, trying to sound as if nothing was wrong.

"Lots of them!" Sid said proudly. "I use only nature's best."

It looks as if Sid *is* a suspect, Nancy thought. She just had to ask him one more question to be sure. "Were you in the park earlier today?"

"No." Sid chuckled. "I've been *here* all day. Making fresh ice cream takes a long time." Then he gave Nancy a big grin.

"Just checking." Nancy said, and skipped back to the table. "Sid couldn't have taken our lemons," she said to her friends. "He's been at the Double Dip all day."

"That's a relief," Bess said, finishing up the last of her ice cream.

"Yeah." George giggled. "If Sid went to jail for stealing our lemons, who'd make our ice cream?"

After Nancy and George had finished their lemonade supreme, the three girls waved goodbye to Sid and went out into the hot afternoon sun. They didn't know what to do next. Their whole day was ruined.

"I guess we could go back to the park," George said. "We can always play on the swings."

"And watch Brenda and Alison sell lemonade?" Bess said. "No way."

"And watch our number one suspects, you mean," Nancy said. "Come on."

At the playground Nancy, Bess, and George sat on the swings. They had a clear view of Brenda and Alison's stand.

"They sure are selling a lot of lemonade," Bess said.

George swung back and forth on her swing. "I'll bet she's hiding our lemons under that tablecloth."

As the girls watched, more and more people lined up to buy lemonade from Brenda and Alison.

A mother with three little girls bought some. Two old men were drinking lemonade, too. And four dog-walkers were patiently waiting their turn. Brenda and Alison were pouring cup after cup.

"We have to think of a way to get a look under their table," Nancy said, starting to swing.

Then Bess started. "I can swing higher than you can, George," Bess sang. "I can see the people by the picnic tables."

"No, you can't," George said, laughing. "I'm swinging so high, I can see the kids on the baseball field."

"I can go higher than both of you." Nancy pushed as hard as she could. Her reddish blond hair flew out behind her as she swung up. "Hey, I see Ned," she called. She brushed her feet against the dirt to slow her swing.

"He has four teeny tiny poodles with him," Bess said. "They're soooo cute."

But it looked as if Ned didn't think the poodles were very cute right then. They were yipping and running around, getting their leashes tangled around his legs.

"He's buying lemonade from Brenda!" George said, pointing.

Brenda helped him untangle the poodles' leashes. Then Ned bought a second cup.

"Let's talk to him before he leaves the park," Nancy said, stopping her swing.

They waited until Ned and the poodles left Brenda's stand. "Wait up!" Nancy yelled to him.

Ned looked over at Nancy, Bess, and George, but he didn't stop. Nancy called louder, but Ned started walking faster.

"Why won't he talk to us?" Bess asked as they followed him out of the park.

"Wait up!" Nancy called again.

Ned turned around angrily. The poodles yelped and jumped excitedly at his legs. "Stop following me!"

"Why are you so mad?" Nancy asked when she finally caught up with him.

"I don't like being followed by pesty girls," Ned said. Now the poodles were running in circles around his feet.

Nancy tightened her lips. "That's a mean thing to say," she said. "Did you know someone stole our lemons?"

"Nope," Ned said, trying to untangle the leashes. "Who would steal your stupid lemons?"

Bess crossed her arms. "That's what we'd like to know."

"I don't know who took them." Ned started walking away. Then he looked over his shoulder. "And stop bothering me!"

26

"We didn't do anything to you!" Nancy shouted.

Ned spun around. "Remember the dogs I was walking this morning?" he asked.

Nancy nodded.

"The owner had told me not to get them dirty because they were just groomed," he continued. "They were so wet and muddy from jumping in the lake after Chip that the owner fired me. Now I'm losing a dollar a day because of you!" Ned led the poodles away from the girls.

"That's terrible," Bess said after he had left. "But it wasn't our fault."

Nancy watched as Ned quickly walked along the street. Halfway down the block, he had to bend down and untangle the four little poodles' leashes again. When he straightened up, Nancy gasped. A bunch of lemon slices had fallen right out of his shirt pocket.

"He's got our lemons!" George cried. "Let's get him!"

4

Fresh-Squeezed Lie

Nancy, Bess, and George raced after Ned. He saw them, picked up the four tiny poodles, and ran away.

"He had . . . too much of a . . . head start," George said to Nancy, out of breath. They had stopped running.

Bess came up after them. "Why didn't you guys wait for me?" she asked, panting.

"We wanted to catch Ned," Nancy said. "But he was too fast." She looked at her watch. "It's getting late. We'd better go home."

"But what about Brenda and Alison?" George asked. "They could have stolen our lemons, too."

"Don't worry," Nancy said to her. "If they took our lemons, they'll want to use them. We'll catch Brenda and Alison tomorrow."

As Nancy sat on the porch, waiting for her father to come home from work, she looked at the "Missing Lemons Mystery" page in her detective's notebook. Finding Ned with that lemon was weird, Nancy thought.

"Another mystery, pudding pie?" Nancy looked up from her notebook to see her father standing in front of her. She jumped up and gave him a big hug.

"Oh, Daddy," she said, "something awful has happened."

Carson Drew led Nancy into the house. "Tell me all about it, pumpkin."

At dinner Nancy explained the mystery, the lemonade-selling contest, and everything that had happened.

"And the worst thing, Daddy," she said, wiping her mouth with her napkin, "is that if we don't get our lemons back, we'll lose the contest. And Brenda and Alison will make us eat bugs!"

"Well, I hear bugs have a lot of vitamins," Carson Drew said with a laugh.

"Daddy!" Nancy said. "This is serious."

"I know, pumpkin. I'll help you buy some more lemons. If Brenda and Alison took them, they won't expect you to be selling lemonade tomorrow."

"Dessert!" Hannah called, coming into the dining room with a pie. "It's delicious and maybe even good for you."

"Are there any bugs in it?" Carson asked Hannah, giving Nancy a wink.

"Bugs?" Hannah said with a huff. "Not in my lemon meringue pie!"

Nancy and her father burst out laughing.

Later Nancy phoned Bess and George with the plan. That evening they made a fancy brand-new sign—much nicer than Alison and Brenda's. It had a large sparkle-painted lemon with drops of juice coming out and glitter all over it.

Early the next morning Hannah woke Nancy up with some good news.

"Look what I found on the porch when I went out to get the newspaper," Hannah said. She was holding a bag from Greenfield's grocery store. It was filled to the top with lemons. "It came with a note." Hannah handed Nancy a piece of paper.

Nancy read it:

> Sorry this bag isn't as big as your box of lemons. It's the best I could do.
>
> The Lemon Stealer

This is a strange clue, Nancy thought as she folded the paper and stuck it in her detective's notebook. Why would the lemon stealer feel bad about stealing?

After breakfast Nancy put on her favorite blue bathing suit underneath her shorts and T-shirt. Hannah had promised to take the girls swimming in the lake that afternoon.

When Bess and George got to Nancy's house, Nancy grabbed Chip's leash, and they were off to the park. On the way, Nancy told them about the note.

"Brenda and Alison actually felt *guilty?*" George said, pulling the wagon behind her. "I don't believe it."

"Why else would they leave us a bag of lemons?" Bess said. "They took our box, and now they're sorry."

"But we don't know that for sure," Nancy said. "Ned's a suspect, too."

Bess looked at the bulky bag lying in the wagon. "Well, at least we have *these.*"

"Yeah, but I still want to find out who stole the other ones," George said.

Nancy thought of her special notebook. She had stuck it in the wagon. "Don't worry, George. We will."

The girls got to the park so early that Brenda and Alison weren't even there yet. They quickly set up their card table with the pink tablecloth, hung

33

their glittery sign, and set out the pitcher and the paper cups.

When Brenda and Alison arrived, Nancy and her friends already had customers. Brenda's mouth dropped open when she saw them.

"Do you see the way they're staring?" Bess said. "They thought they wouldn't see us here again."

"Well, if they try anything funny, we'll be waiting," George said. "They won't get away with stealing our lemons twice."

The rest of the morning, Nancy, Bess, and George sold so much lemonade that they didn't have time to think about the mystery. Bobby Alden even bought two cups.

"You stop by our stand almost as often as we go to the Double Dip," Nancy said to Bobby as she poured his second cup.

Bobby laughed. "I have a secret." He leaned in closer. "I come to the park every time I run an errand for my

grandfather. Right now I'm on my way back to the shop."

"Does Sid know?" Bess asked.

"Nope." Bobby picked up his cup. "I'm supposed to go straight back, so don't tell him, okay?"

"Okay," Nancy said as he walked away.

For a while, nobody came to their table. Nancy looked over at Brenda and Alison's stand. No one was there, either.

"It's time to find out if Brenda and Alison have our lemons," Nancy said.

"But they'll never let us near their stuff." Bess poured herself a cup of lemonade. "Ah, scrumptious," she said after taking a gulp.

"I know what we can do," Nancy said, pouring herself and George some, too. "We'll walk Chip over to Brenda and Alison's stand. Then I'll let go of Chip's leash, and she'll run around. I'll search under their table when they're not looking."

"Sounds ingenious," George said, touching her cup to Nancy's.

"I'll stay here, just in case," Bess said. "We wouldn't want anything to happen to our new lemons."

"Good thinking, Bess." Nancy picked up Chip's leash. "Come on, George. Let's snoop!"

Nancy and George walked Chip past Brenda and Alison's table.

"Great stand, Brenda," George said sweetly, looking at their Fresh-Squeezed Lemonade sign. "Wasn't it a good idea to have a contest?"

"Especially since we're winning," Alison said. She bent down and pretended to look through the grass. "What kind of bugs do you guys like?"

"Oh, I don't know." Nancy let go of Chip's leash. The puppy jumped up on Alison and started licking her face.

"Yecch, doggy kisses!" Alison yelled. She pushed Chip away. Then, before anyone had a chance to do anything, Chip darted underneath the table. A second later she scurried out, holding several paper packets in her mouth.

Brenda tried to grab them, but Chip

ran over to Nancy. Then Chip shook her head, and the packets burst open. As Brenda groaned, Nancy took the torn envelopes out of Chip's mouth and frowned.

"Dirty, rotten cheaters," she said. "This is lemonade mix!"

5

Ned Tells the Truth

Your sign is a big lie!" George shouted. "You aren't using fresh-squeezed lemons at all!"

"It's not a lie!" Brenda held up an empty box. "See? It says, 'Tastes like fresh-squeezed lemonade.' "

"You're still cheating," George said.

"No, we're not." Alison raised her nose in the air. "We're just saying what it says on the package."

"Besides"—Brenda gave George and Nancy a sneaky smile—"nobody *said* we had to use fresh lemons for the contest."

Without saying a word, Nancy

grabbed Chip's leash and headed back to the stand. She and George had taken only a few steps when they heard Alison say to Brenda, "That dog ruined all of our lemonade mix. Now we have to go buy some more."

George grinned. "Chocolate Chip sure is smart."

The two girls laughed all the way back to their stand.

"This means Brenda and Alison aren't suspects anymore," Bess said when Nancy and George told her about the mix.

"They're still suspects," George said. "They want to win the contest, right?"

"They would have won, too, if someone hadn't bought us these." Bess took a lemon from their bag and started squeezing it.

"Wait a minute," Nancy said suddenly. "Brenda and Alison *can't* be suspects."

"Why not?" George asked.

"You said it yourself," Nancy said. "Brenda and Alison want to win the contest. So why would they steal our lemons and then buy us more? It doesn't make sense."

"They felt guilty?" Bess said with a smile.

George looked at her cousin. "Yeah, maybe . . . *not!*"

"Those lemons had to come from Ned. He's the only suspect left," Nancy said. "We have to talk to him. But I haven't seen him at all today."

"He probably feels too guilty to come around here," George said.

"I can't think about this anymore." Bess rubbed her stomach. "I'm starving."

"We forgot to bring lunch," Nancy said. "But we can't go home. Now that Brenda and Alison are at the store, we have a chance to win the contest."

George grinned. "Let's have ice cream for lunch!"

"I heard that," a voice said from behind them. It was Hannah. She was carrying a cooler. "I figured you girls were working hard. So I brought you—"

"Lunch!" The three girls attacked

41

the cooler. Inside were chicken salad sandwiches, oatmeal cookies, and a peach for each of them.

The girls sat down on the grass to eat.

"We don't have anything to drink, Hannah," Nancy said, munching on her sandwich.

Bess and George stopped eating and looked at her.

"Just kidding." Nancy giggled. She went over to the table and brought back the big pitcher of lemonade.

"Don't eat too much," Hannah said. "You're going swimming soon."

"But who's going to guard our stand and take care of Chip?" George asked.

"I'll do it," Bess said. "I don't like swimming that much."

Nancy remembered the time she and Bess had gone to Camp Treehouse. Bess hadn't wanted to go swimming even then. "We'll do something really special for you later," she said.

After the girls had rested awhile after lunch, Hannah walked Nancy and

George over to the lake and sat down near the lifeguard.

The girls saw some of their friends jumping off the floating dock.

"Come on," Katie Zaleski called to them before she plunged into the water.

"Race you!" Nancy shouted to George as they jumped in.

"I beat you," George said, laughing as she touched the wooden dock first.

Nancy dunked herself under the water. She came up really fast and pushed a wave at her friend. "Gotcha!"

George did the same thing back. She hit Peter DeSands with water, too, and Nancy laughed. Then Peter tried to splash George but got little Jimmy Koombs instead. Jimmy started crying, and Mrs. Koombs had to come in to get him.

"Let's go over to the tire swing and jump off," Nancy said.

"Sure." George started to swim.

The girls swam as fast as they could to a big tire hanging over the water from a tree branch.

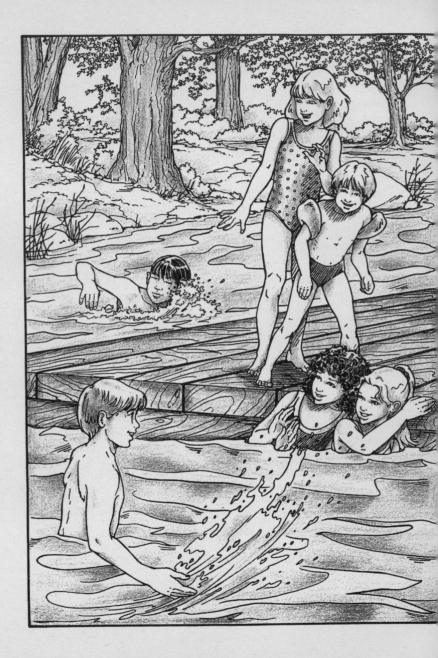

"Let's rest here for a minute," George said, floating on her back. "But stay away from the prickly bushes along the lakeshore."

When Nancy looked at the bushes with the light green leaves, something yellow caught her eye. "Wait a minute," she said, and swam a little closer to the edge of the lake. George followed her.

There, floating near the prickly bushes, they found some fat, mushy lemons.

"There's a whole bunch of them," George said. "I'll bet they're ours."

"But why would the lemon stealer throw them in the lake?" Nancy asked.

Just then she heard growling behind her. Nancy and George turned around quickly and saw Ned standing by the shore. He had another pack of dogs with him.

"Look," he said. "I just want to apologize for taking your lemons."

6

Supreme Suspect

I knew it!" George said right away.

"I didn't think it was any big deal," Ned said, trying to hold on to his dogs.

"No big deal?" Nancy said. "We might totally lose a contest with Brenda and Alison because of you!"

"Look, I said I was sorry." Ned turned to leave.

"Why did you buy us a new bag of lemons after you threw our old ones in the lake?" Nancy asked.

"What are you talking about?" Ned said, turning back around.

"Those." Nancy pointed to the lemons floating near the prickly bushes.

"I didn't do that," Ned said. "And I didn't buy you a new bag, either." He bent down to pet a cocker spaniel.

"I only took a couple of lemons because the golden retriever liked them so much," he continued. "She started obeying me when I gave her a couple of slices. Now I use them as treats. Some of my dogs don't like them, but these do. See?"

Ned took some lemon slices out of his shirt pocket and fed them to the dogs. They quickly gobbled up the sour fruit.

"Did you see anybody near our stand when you were walking out of the park?" George asked.

Ned nodded. "I saw a lot of people near your stand. But the only one I knew was Bobby Alden." He stood up and handed some more slices to the dogs. "But he didn't have anything with him except a box of ice cream."

"Oh," Nancy said sadly. She thought for sure that either Ned or Brenda and

Alison had stolen the lemons. Now it was clear that they weren't guilty.

"Well, I've got to get these dogs back to their owners. Sorry about raiding your lemon box, Nancy." Ned walked away.

George scrambled out of the lake. "I don't feel like jumping from the tire swing anymore."

"Me neither," Nancy said, carefully making her way to the prickly bushes. "But I'm going to grab one of those squishy lemons. It could be a clue."

When Nancy and George were back on shore, Hannah walked them to the stand and said goodbye. "Don't be late for dinner," she said to Nancy as she headed out of the park.

"I'm going to get you a special treat for staying here while George and I went swimming," Nancy said to Bess.

"What is it?" Bess said, jumping up and down.

"You'll see," Nancy said.

*   *   *

"Hi, Sid," Nancy said when she walked into the Double Dip.

Sid Alden was scooping lemonade supreme ice cream into a cone for a customer. "Back again so soon?" he asked.

"I need three cups of ice cream: a scoop of fudge ripple for me, one scoop of chocolate for George, and a special peanut butter cup sundae for Bess," Nancy said.

"I wonder where Bobby is," Sid said, giving the other customer his change.

Nancy didn't say anything.

"I've been so busy," Sid continued, "and Bobby always seems to disappear just at the wrong moment."

Nancy thought about her promise to Bobby. She wasn't going to tell Sid that Bobby hung out in the park sometimes. But she didn't like keeping a secret from him.

As Sid squirted chocolate syrup onto the peanut butter cup ice cream, Nancy looked at all the other flavors through the glass display case. Then something caught her eye.

There, behind the counter, she saw a box of lemons! Nancy's mouth fell open.

"Something wrong?" Sid asked.

Nancy looked up quickly. "Uh, I was just wondering where you got that box from."

Sid plopped a cherry on top of Bess's sundae. "Lemonade supreme is doing so well," he said, "that I sent Bobby to Greenfield's to buy some more lemons."

Nancy's heart sank. The box wasn't hers. It was hopeless. She was never going to solve this mystery.

Sid looked at Nancy. "I know something's wrong." He walked around the display case and bent over, his hands on his knees. "Tell me about it."

"I thought that box of lemons was mine," Nancy said in a tiny voice. She told Sid all about the mystery.

"I'm sorry, Nancy," Sid said, touching her chin. "Will some more free ice cream make you feel better?"

Nancy looked up at Sid. He's even nicer than Santa Claus, she thought.

The little bell on the front door rang. Bobby walked into the ice-cream shop.

"It's about time, Bobby," Sid said to his grandson. "Take this delivery bag to Mrs. Cranford's house—and quick. It's for a party."

Bobby took the big bag from his grandfather. It had Double Dip printed on it in fancy pink letters.

Then Sid handed Nancy the three cups of ice cream in a fancy bag, too.

"Thanks, Sid!" Nancy said. "I feel better already."

Back at the park, Nancy, Bess, and George ate their ice cream and quickly went back to work squeezing lemons.

No sooner were they covered with juice than Brenda walked up to them.

"You guys are working hard for nothing." Brenda laughed, pointing at the sticky mess on their table. "Alison and I are going to win."

"Why don't you just go back to your own stand?" Bess said.

"Okay, but at five o'clock today, we'll

find out who's going to eat bugs," Brenda said.

"Or worse!" Nancy shouted as Brenda walked away. She took a lemon from the grocery bag. She wanted to throw it at Brenda, but she didn't. Instead she cut it in half and put it on the juicer.

As she squeezed the lemon, Nancy thought of something Sid had said. He had told Nancy that his box of lemons was from Greenfield's grocery. Nancy looked down at her sack. Greenfield's lemons came in bags, not boxes!

Nancy stood up so fast she almost knocked over the juice she had worked so hard to squeeze.

"What's going on, Nancy?" George asked, startled.

Nancy was so angry she couldn't hold it in any longer. "Sid Alden is a liar!"

7

A Smelly Clue

"Sid, a liar?" Bess said. "Impossible!"

"He gave us free ice cream twice," George added. "A liar wouldn't do that."

"Maybe there was a reason he gave us all that ice cream," Nancy said. Then she explained how she had seen the box of lemons at the Double Dip.

"He said the box was from Greenfield's," she continued. "But it couldn't be."

"You're right," George said. "My mom always gets lemons from Greenfield's. And they're always in bags."

"Sid definitely could have bought us

the new lemons," Bess added. "A kid might not have had enough money."

By the sad looks on Bess's and George's faces, Nancy could tell her friends were convinced. "We have to go to the Double Dip and get our box. Then we'll have proof," Nancy said.

"But, Nancy," Bess said, "if we stop selling lemonade now, Brenda and Alison will win the contest."

"This contest is over," Brenda said loudly as she and Alison walked up. They were carrying their jar full of quarters.

"Let's count the money," Alison said.

For the next fifteen minutes, both teams counted their quarters. Then they counted again to make sure they were right the first time.

"Alison and I made fourteen dollars and seventy-five cents," Brenda announced. "Beat that."

Nancy was almost finished counting the money out loud for the second time. "Fourteen dollars and fifty cents . . . seventy-five cents . . ." Then she looked up and plunked down the last quarter. "Fifteen dollars!"

"We won! We won!" Nancy, Bess, and George screamed together. They hugged one another and jumped up and down in a circle. "Yay!"

"No!" Brenda shouted. "I'm not going to eat a bug."

"Me neither," Alison said, looking worried.

"Don't worry," Bess said, giving them a big fake smile. "We're going to make you do something much worse."

"Meet us by the big oak tree at noon tomorrow," George said. "Or else."

Brenda and Alison looked at each other and frowned.

"We'll be there," Brenda said, but she didn't sound happy.

Nancy, Bess, and George packed their things in the wagon.

"What are we going to make Brenda and Alison do?" Bess asked.

"I don't know," Nancy said, "but it has to be *really* gross."

All the way home, the girls tried to

think of something awful enough for Brenda and Alison. But when they reached Nancy's house, they still hadn't decided. The three friends unloaded the wagon and carried everything into the kitchen.

"We're going to the Double Dip," Nancy told Hannah.

"I don't think that's a good idea," Hannah said. "It's very close to dinnertime."

"Please, Hannah? We just need to talk to Sid. We won't eat any ice cream," Nancy promised.

"Okay. But be back in half an hour, Nancy," Hannah said.

On the way to the shop the girls talked about the case.

"I can't believe Sid took our lemons," George said.

"Yeah." Nancy kicked a pebble.

"The Double Dip's been so crowded," Bess said, "you'd think he'd be too busy to go around stealing from kids."

"What did you say, Bess?" Nancy asked.

"I said that Sid was really busy," Bess answered. "Why?"

Nancy snapped her fingers. "Sid *was* really busy," Nancy said. "He even told me he was at the Double Dip making ice cream when our lemons were stolen."

"But he could be lying," George said.

"I don't think he is," Nancy said. "I haven't seen him in the park at all. Have you guys?"

Bess and George shook their heads.

"And making that ice cream takes time," Bess said. "Right?"

"But then who did steal the lemons?" George asked.

"Well, I have an idea," Nancy said slowly. "But I'm not sure."

The girls walked silently until they reached the door to the ice-cream shop.

"I can't take it anymore, Nancy," Bess said suddenly. "You have to tell us who you think it is."

Nancy turned to her friends. "The more I think about it, the more the clues point to Bobby," she said. "He was around our stand a lot. He works at the Double Dip, so he could have put the box behind the counter. He's nice enough to feel guilty and buy us extra lemons. And he has a job, so he could pay for them."

"I just remembered something," George said. "Ned said that he saw Bobby carrying a box of ice cream. Maybe that box didn't have ice cream in it. Maybe it was full of lemons instead!"

"The only thing left to do is see if that box is ours." Nancy sighed. "If it is, that proves Bobby stole it."

"But he bought our lemonade," Bess said. "Why would he steal from us?"

"That's what we're going to find out," Nancy said. "Here's the plan. You and George keep Bobby and Sid busy. I'll see if I can find that box."

When they walked into the ice-cream shop, Sid was behind the counter, setting up for the after-dinner rush. He was carrying tubs of ice cream from the big freezers in the back of the shop and putting them in the display case.

Nancy peeked through the glass case at the spot where she had seen the box of lemons earlier. It wasn't there. How am I going to get a chance to snoop? she wondered. Then out loud, she said, "Where's Bobby?"

"Bobby went on an errand," Sid answered. "He'll be back in a few minutes."

"I need a peanut butter cup sundae with sprinkles," Bess said, trying to keep Sid from going into the back of the shop.

"Didn't you already have ice cream today?" Sid asked.

"Just one teeny-weeny scoop," Bess said. "Please?" She gave Sid her sweetest smile.

Sid laughed and put a very small scoop of ice cream into a cup.

"How come you put the ice cream in the big freezers at night?" George asked. "Isn't this counter freezer cold enough?"

Good thinking, George, Nancy said

to herself. Sid loved talking about that stuff.

While Sid told Bess and George about how different temperatures affect ice cream, Nancy quietly slipped down a short hallway. She walked to the back of the restaurant and opened the door to the storage room. There were no lemon boxes there.

Then she tiptoed out the back door into the alley and saw a big green metal Dumpster with the top open. Maybe the box is in there, Nancy thought. She pulled a wooden crate close to the Dumpster and climbed up for a better look.

This is really smelly, Nancy thought, holding her nose. But she knew she had to look inside. All the really good detectives on TV went through garbage to find clues.

Then Nancy smiled. Right on top was the cardboard box. Nancy reached in. Just as she grabbed the box, she heard a loud voice.

"What do you think you're doing?"

8

Grosser than Gross

Bobby was standing in the alley, holding a Greenfield's grocery bag.

Nancy lowered the box back into the Dumpster so Bobby couldn't see it.

"You could get hurt up there, Nancy," Bobby said. "Let me help you down."

Nancy didn't want his help. She didn't want him to see her with the box until she could make sure it was hers.

"Do you always go through other people's garbage?" He moved closer. "What are you doing, anyway?"

Nancy had to think fast. If Bobby came any nearer he'd see the box.

"Uh, garbage can be really interesting," Nancy answered quickly.

"Garbage, interesting?" Bobby repeated.

"Yes, um, I mean, I think I lost something in here," Nancy said. "And it would be *interesting* if I found it."

Bobby frowned and shook his head.

"Sometimes you're a strange kid, Nancy," he muttered. "Well, I'd better take this stuff inside. My grandpa's waiting."

Now Nancy had a chance to look at the box carefully. It was addressed to the Drew family. The box was hers!

Nancy raced into the shop. Bobby looked as if he was about to leave, but she held out the box toward him. "Where did you get this box, Bobby?" she asked loudly.

George and Bess were sitting at one of the little tables.

Sid looked up. "Oh, you're still interested in that box from Greenfield's."

Bobby stopped short, but he didn't turn around.

"Is it really from Greenfield's, Bobby?" Nancy asked.

"How should I know?" Bobby said. "All cardboard boxes look alike."

"What's going on here?" Sid asked. He looked at Bobby, then at Nancy.

"Remember when I told you someone took our lemons?" Nancy asked Sid.

Sid nodded.

"We think it was Bobby." Nancy walked over to where Bess and George were sitting.

"Why would I do that?" Bobby asked.

"I don't know," Nancy answered. "But if you didn't, how did our box end up in your Dumpster?"

"That's the box they gave me at Greenfield's!" Bobby yelled.

"Enough!" Sid shouted, making everyone stop talking. Then he looked at Nancy. "What makes you think that's your box?" he asked gently.

"This," Nancy said. She handed Sid the box and showed him the label. "It's addressed to my family. My father's friend in California sent us a whole box of lemons from his very own trees."

Sid took a deep breath and looked at his grandson. "What's the meaning of this, Bobby?"

Bobby turned bright red. "You're right, Nancy," he said. "I did take your lemons. I had to."

"You'd better explain right now, young man," Sid said.

"You gave me money and sent me to the store to buy extra lemons for lemonade supreme," Bobby started to explain. "And I bought them from Greenfield's grocery store. It was so hot and such a nice day," Bobby continued. "I stopped at the park—"

"I told you to come right back," Sid interrupted.

Bobby looked at his sneakers. "I put the bag down on the shore of the lake and went for a swim. While I was swimming, the bag fell into the water."

Nancy remembered the floating yellow lemons by the prickly bushes.

"I knew you would be mad at me."

Bobby looked up at his grandfather. "So later, when all the dogs started running around, I took Nancy's lemons."

"Didn't you think we'd mind?" George asked.

"I knew you would. That's why I bought more right away with my own money," Bobby said. "I left them on Nancy's porch that night."

"Thank you," Nancy said, "even though you took them in the first place."

"I'm glad you repaid these girls," Sid said to Bobby. "But that doesn't make up for stealing."

Bobby looked at Nancy, Bess, and George. "I'm really sorry," he said. "Is there anything I can do to make it up to you?"

Nancy knew that Bobby really meant it. She remembered the note from the lemon stealer. Bobby was sorry even before she solved the mystery, she thought.

"Well, since you gave us the other lemons, I guess it's okay."

"Wait a minute." Bess stood up. "There *is* something you could do for us, Bobby."

George looked at her cousin and giggled. "Yeah, something *gross*. . . ."

The next day at noon Nancy, Bess, and George met Brenda and Alison at the big oak tree.

"Let's get this over with," Brenda said.

"Anything but a worm," Alison said, squirming.

"We said it was going to be grosser than eating a bug," George said.

Then Bess went behind the tree. When she came back out, Bobby was with her. "You both have to kiss him," she said, bringing Bobby closer to Brenda and Alison.

"On the lips," Nancy added with a sly smile.

Brenda and Alison looked at each other. "Eeeeewwwwww!"

*　　*　　*

That evening Nancy sat on her porch with her blue notebook. She turned to her latest mystery page and wrote:

The Missing Lemon Mystery— Solved!

Bobby Alden did the wrong thing, but he made up for it as soon as he could.

Brenda and Alison should never have gotten into a contest where the loser has to do anything the winner says. Because my best friends and I can think up things that are *grosser* than gross.

Case closed.

THE NANCY DREW NOTEBOOKS®

by Carolyn Keene
Illustrated by Anthony Accardo

Simon & Schuster Mail Order Dept. BWB
200 Old Tappan Rd., Old Tappan, N.J. 07675

A MINSTREL BOOK
Published by Pocket Books

Please send me the books I have checked above. I am enclosing $_____ (please add $0.75 to cover the postage and handling for each order. Please add appropriate sales tax). Send check or money order--no cash or C.O.D.'s please. Allow up to six weeks for delivery. For purchase over $10.00 you may use VISA: card number, expiration date and customer signature must be included.

Name _____

Address _____

City _____ State/Zip _____

VISA Card # _____ Exp.Date _____

Signature _____ 1045-13

TAKE A RIDE
WITH THE KIDS ON BUS FIVE!

Natalie Adams and James Penny have just started
third grade. They like their teacher, and they like
Maple Street School. The only trouble is, they have
to ride bad old Bus Five to get there!

#1 THE BAD NEWS BULLY
Can Natalie and James stop the bully on Bus Five?

#2 WILD MAN AT THE WHEEL
When Mr. Balter calls in sick,
the kids get some strange new drivers.

#3 FINDERS KEEPERS
The kids on Bus Five keep losing things.
Is there a thief on board?

#4 I SURVIVED ON BUS FIVE
Bad luck turns into big fun
when Bus Five breaks down in a rainstorm.

BY MARCIA LEONARD
ILLUSTRATED BY JULIE DURRELL

 A MINSTREL® BOOK

Published by Pocket Books

1237-04

FULL HOUSE™
Michelle

#1: THE GREAT PET PROJECT 51905-0/$3.50
#2: THE SUPER-DUPER SLEEPOVER PARTY
51906-9/$3.50
#3: MY TWO BEST FRIENDS 52271-X/$3.99
#4: LUCKY, LUCKY DAY 52272-8/$3.50
#5: THE GHOST IN MY CLOSET 53573-0/$3.99
#6: BALLET SURPRISE 53574-9/$3.99
#7: MAJOR LEAGUE TROUBLE 53575-7/$3.99
#8: MY FOURTH-GRADE MESS 53576-5/$3.99
#9: BUNK 3, TEDDY, AND ME 56834-5/$3.99
#10: MY BEST FRIEND IS A MOVIE STAR!
(Super Edition) 56835-3/$3.99
#11: THE BIG TURKEY ESCAPE 56836-1/$3.99
#12: THE SUBSTITUTE TEACHER 00364-X/$3.99
#13: CALLING ALL PLANETS 00365-8/$3.50
#14: I'VE GOT A SECRET 00366-6/$3.99
#15: HOW TO BE COOL 00833-1/$3.99

A MINSTREL® BOOK
Published by Pocket Books

Simon & Schuster Mail Order Dept. BWB
200 Old Tappan Rd., Old Tappan, N.J. 07675

Please send me the books I have checked above. I am enclosing $_____(please add $0.75 to cover the postage and handling for each order. Please add appropriate sales tax). Send check or money order--no cash or C.O.D.'s please. Allow up to six weeks for delivery. For purchase over $10.00 you may use VISA: card number, expiration date and customer signature must be included.

Name _____

Address _____

City _____ State/Zip _____

VISA Card # _____ Exp. Date _____

Signature _____

1033-19